**DENNY
PRIMARY
SCHOOL**

For Lily, Edmund and Laurence.

Teddy Bears have such a quiet life,
don't they?

Scholastic Children's Books,
Commonwealth House, 1-19 New Oxford Street,
London WC1A 1NU, UK
a division of Scholastic Ltd

London ~ New York ~ Toronto ~ Sydney ~ Auckland

Published by Scholastic Ltd, 1997

Text and illustrations copyright © Ian Beck, 1997

ISBN 0 590 54227 X (Hardback)
ISBN 0 590 19918 8 (Paperback)

Printed and bound in Hong Kong

The right of Ian Beck to be identified as the author and illustrator of this work
has been asserted by him in accordance with the Copyright, Designs and Patents Act, 1988.

Teddy was sitting alone on the stairs. Lily and her Mum were getting ready to go out.

"Wait," said Lily. "We can't go yet, we nearly forgot Teddy. Poor old thing, he thought he was left behind."

"Oooh, it's windy," said Mum. "I'm glad we're wrapped up warm."
"Teddy likes going to the park," said Lily.

They stayed a long time in the park. They
played on the swings, and they fed the ducks.

"It's getting late," said Mum, "and I think it might rain. Come on, we must get home before dark."

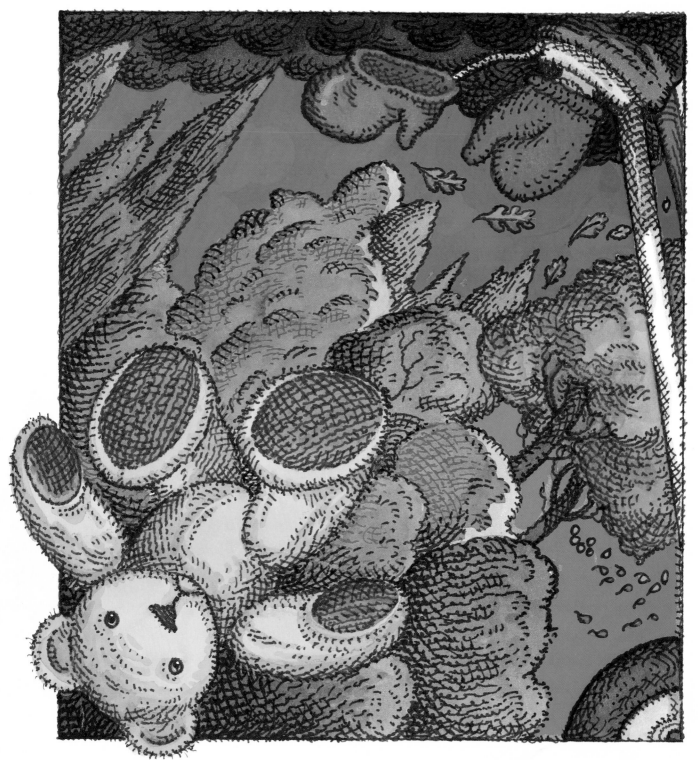

Lily was so tired she fell asleep. She cuddled Teddy but . . . Oh no, poor Teddy, Lily dropped him!

And so Mum and Lily set off home
without Teddy.

Teddy was left all alone.

He walked up to the dark iron railings.

And he pushed, and squeezed, and squashed up
his tummy until . . .

. . . he was through. But out on the
pavement he felt VERY small.

Then it began to rain. And the rain came down harder and harder.

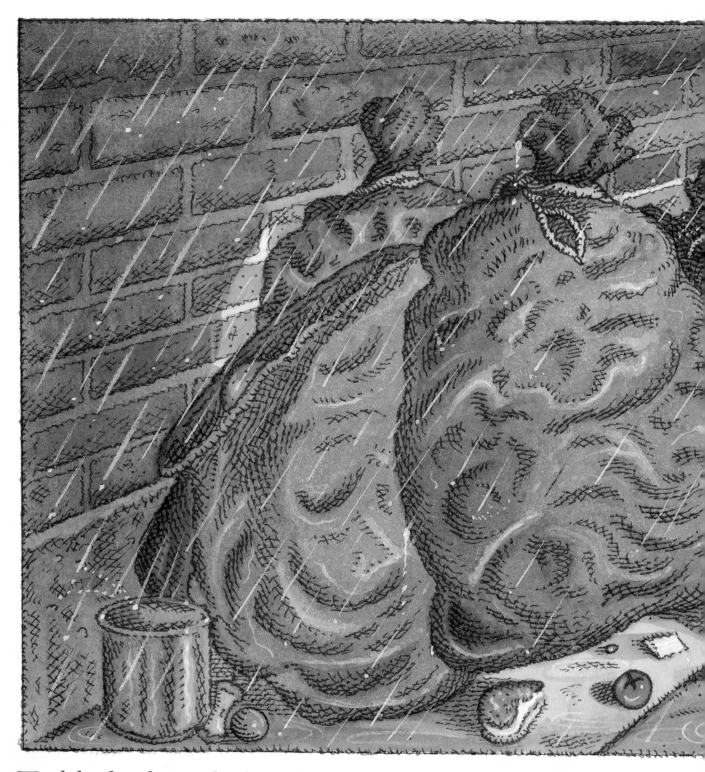

Teddy had to shelter by a dustbin. A great, big, hairy dog came and sniffed at him.

Teddy thought that he would never
see Lily again.

"I MUST get home before dark. That's when Lily needs me the most." So bravely he set off up the hill against the wind and the rain.

It was a very, very, VERY steep hill. By the time he reached the top, it was nearly dark.

And it was a very, very, VERY strong wind.

"WHOOSH!" went the wind. Head over heels he tumbled, down and over, over and down, all the way to his house.

He tried to tap at the door with his cold, wet paws, but no one could hear him.

And so out in the dark, he waited, and waited,
and waited . . .

Until a friendly voice said, "You poor old bear, have they forgotten you? Never mind, I know what to do."

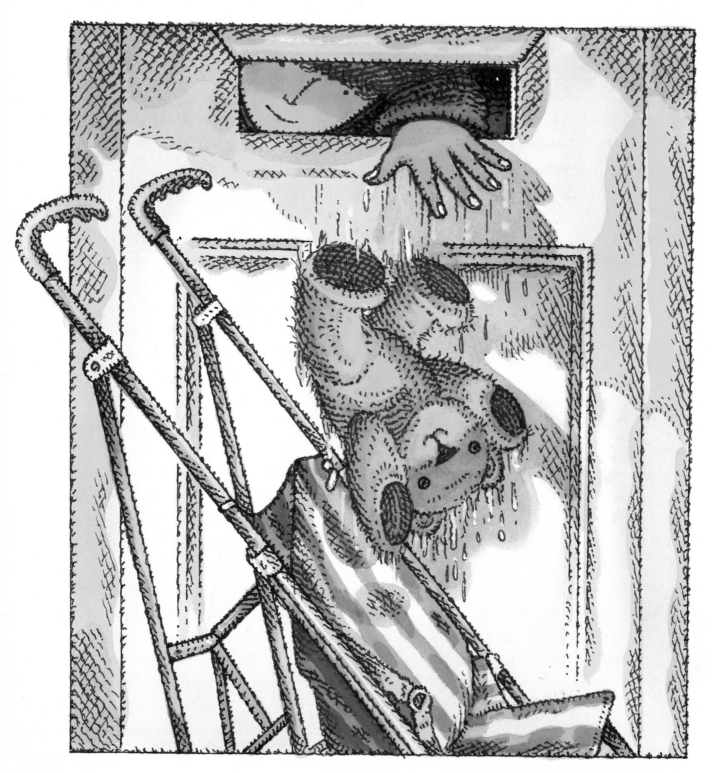

And so the paperboy delivered Teddy through
the letter box, into the warmth and safety of
the buggy seat.

At bedtime, Lily said, "Where's Teddy? I can't go to bed without him. Ah, here he is. You have an easy life, don't you Teddy?"

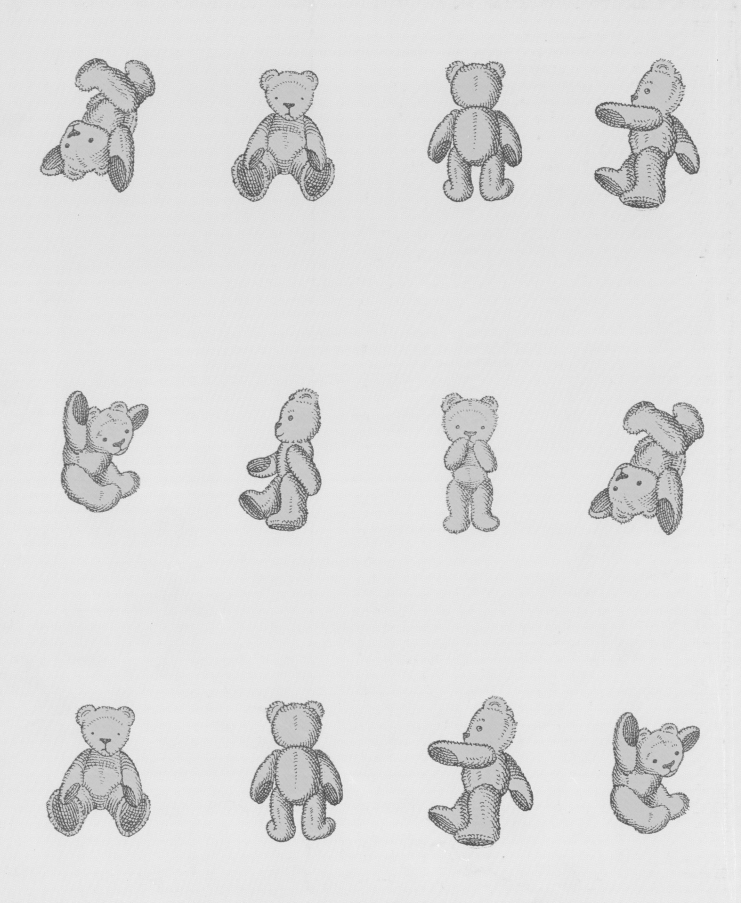